Arlo The Ant
And His Very
Big Red Pants

Published by
Kindle Direct Publishing [KDP]
www.nannibooks.com

Arlo the ant wore his very big pants every day.
They were red in colour and tied at the waist with a long piece of
yellow string.

Arlo loved his red pants, they had lots of pockets to put things in.
Big pockets and small pockets, on the back and on the front,
on his knees and at the side.
Every day he filled all his pockets with all sorts of bits and bobs.
None of which were useful things for ants.

Arlo stuffed his pockets with anything he could find when he was
out playing with his friends. He loved it when they played hide-and-seek,
because he found lots of funny things in the bushes like, bags full of
dog poop, and lots of different colour balls that the big people left behind.

His favorite thing to collect were the shiny bottle tops which came
in all shapes and sizes.

Of course he didn't pick up the dog poop, it was smelly,
"YUK" said Arlo.
Arlo collected all the balls and bottle tops, because he loved to play
with them in his bedroom. He had hundreds of them in all shapes and
sizes. They were under his bed, in his wardrobe and on top of
his wardrobe. They were everywhere and Arlo loved it.

One day, Arlo's mum said he had to go out with the worker ants to collect some food, just like his friends did everyday.

Arlo was very sad, as he couldn't wear his big red pants. He had to wear the green worker ant pants and they had NO POCKETS.

Arlo followed the worker ants to the park
where they always went every day,
to collect food that the big people left behind.

Two of the worker ants,
Barnaby and Birch were his best friends.

"Barnaby, Birch, what do I have to do?"
whispered Arlo so the other worker ants didn't laugh at him.

"Well", replied Barnaby,
"You have to look for food and carry it home on your back".
"Yes", exclaimed Birch, "That's exactly what you have to do!".

"Okay", replied Arlo, wandering off to find some food.
Arlo whooped with joy when he found some juicy orange slices
on the grass.
He tried to lift one up, but it was very heavy and so
he put it down again.

Arlo looked around at the other worker ants to see how they did it.
His eyes went very round when he saw his friends
Barnaby and Birch
carrying a very big apple between them on their backs.

Arlo tried again to pick up the orange and he slowly managed to
slide it onto his back.
The juice from the orange dripped down Arlo's
back and all over his face.
Making him very sticky indeed and very uncomfortable.

"Mmmmmmmmmmmmmm", slurped Arlo "This is great",..
he said to no-one in particular , as he licked the juice that was
dripping down his face.

Arlo started to walk back home slowly, as the orange on his back was very
heavy. He was also becoming very uncomfortable with the dripping juice,
as it was making him sticky all over.
"Maybe this isn't so great after all", Arlo muttered to himself quietly.

Arlo went to bed that night thinking about what he could do to make
carrying the food back home much easier.
As he sat on his bed he saw
his favorite big red pants hanging on the back of the chair.

"I know", he shouted excitedly, "I will wear my very big red pants",
then he got into bed with a very big smile
on his face and went fast asleep.

The next day he went down to breakfast wearing his very big red pants.
"Arlo, why are you wearing those, what happened to your
green worker pants",said his mum.
"You'll see mum", laughed Arlo as he skipped out of the house.

Arlo saw his friends Barnaby and Birch and joined them
as they walked to the Park.

"Why are you wearing your big red pants Arlo? Asked Birch.

"You'll see Birch", answered Arlo.

Arlo went off by himself to find some food and before
long he found some
nuts and biscuits on the floor near the picnic bench.

Arlo was very happy as he picked them up one by one and stuffed them
into the pockets of his very big red pants.

When all his pockets were full, Arlo started to make his way back home.
As he walked home, he came across a big yellow banana.
Arlo knew his mum loved bananas and wanted to take the banana home
but his pockets were full.

"What can I do?", Arlo thought to
himself as he twiddled
with the yellow string
holding up his very big red pants.

Arlo suddenly had a bright idea and stopped playing with
the yellow string,
looking down at it with a big grin on his face.

He went to the banana and tied the yellow string around it tightly.
As he finished tying the string, he looked up and saw Barnaby and Birch
walking past with a big slice of chocolate cake on their backs.

"Hi Barnaby, hi Birch, look at what I've got", Arlo shouted,
as he proudly showed off what he had collected. Barnaby and Birch
looked at him in admiration,
"Your so clever Arlo", they both said at the same time.

With his very big red pants full to bursting, Arlo waddled
home slowly with the banana bumping along the ground behind him.
His friends Barnaby and Birch walked
with him wishing they had big red pants too.

Arlo was greeted with lots of cheers when he got home, thanks to his very big red pants.
"Your so clever Arlo", said his mum, giving him a big hug.
"Thank you for my banana, I really love banana".

The next day when Arlo was going to the park he saw his friends, Barnaby and Birch again. This time they both had big grins on their faces too, as they also wore very big red pants like Arlo.
Arlo and his very big red pants were a very big hit!

" Look out for more books on Arlo the Ant "

Printed in Great Britain
by Amazon

20273896R00016